TO Ann & Jack,

Love

Cici Angel

D1060439

King Leo
and the Feast

Written by **Gigi Amal**

Illustrated by **Theresa Burns**

King Leo LLC
St. Louis, Missouri

Copyright © 2020 King Leo LLC

All rights reserved. No portion of this book may be reproduced mechanically, electronically, or by any other means, including photocopying, without written permission of the publisher. It is illegal to copy this book, post it to a website, or distribute it by any other means without permission from the publisher.

Published by King Leo LLC
St. Louis, Missouri

Order more books and other delightful items about *King Leo and the Feast* at www.GigiAmal.com

Illustrations by Theresa Burns

Art editing by Joe Eckstein, Kaelen Felix, and Michael Stull

Cover and interior design by Joe Eckstein, Imagine! Studios
www.ArtsImagine.com

Scripture quotation taken from the Holy Bible, New International Version®, NIV®. Copyright ©1973, 1978, 1984, 2011 by Biblica, Inc.™ Used by permission of Zondervan. All rights reserved worldwide. www.zondervan.com The "NIV" and "New International Version" are trademarks registered in the United States Patent and Trademark Office by Biblica, Inc.™

ISBN: 978-1-7354444-0-6 (paperback)
ISBN: 978-1-7354444-1-3 (hardback)
ISBN: 978-1-7354444-2-0 (e-book)
ISBN: 978-1-7354444-3-7 (audiobook)

Library of Congress Control Number: 2020945257

Second Printing: May 2021

"Come, all you who are thirsty,

come to the waters . . . "

Isaiah 55:1

Table of Contents

Royal and Quite Regal

There once was a cat who lived in a palace,
Who ate every meal from a crystal chalice!
Whose fur was soft, fluffy and white,
With radiance did glow, a majestic sight!

With eyes that twinkled in the night,
Like flames of fire, burning bright.
Whose collars were of precious jewels,
Emeralds and jasper, sapphires too!

Who wore a brilliant, dazzling crown,
With gems that sparkled all around!
Adorned with robes of crimson red,
Spun with costly golden thread.

Yet loved to laugh and dance and sing,
This cat indeed, was a king!

And every day he would ride,

A carriage of gold, with guards by his side.

To govern and rule his vast estate,

Through meadows and fields, from gate to gate!

And all would come, from far and from near,

To attend and to listen, and to hear.

His words of power and great might,

Filled all who heard, with delight!

King Leo was the name of this cat,

Royal and quite regal, all were certain of that!

On Palace Grounds

One day as King Leo strolled round about,
On palace grounds, inside and out.
All by himself, with no one to share,
The joys and sounds, all without care!

"How I wish I had a companion, a mate,
Someone to share this vast estate.

Two I know, are better than one,
Their joy is double, and so is their fun!
Surely there must be lands to see,
In faraway places, with friends just for me."

So King Leo sat and pondered and mused,
Thinking about, just what to do!
Then all at once, he had a thought,
Something quite simple and having no fraught.

"I will have a magnificent feast,
And invite every cat, from greatest to least.
I will invite, from far and from near,
To come and partake of all I hold dear!"

Joy and Excitement

So off King Leo went, to plan and prepare,
Having not a moment to spare.
"I will serve the greatest of feasts,
And invite every cat, from greatest to least!

Every kind and all sorts of fish,
Mackerel and tuna on every dish!
An abundance of fruit, from which to choose,
Mulberries and mangoes and papayas too!

Nuts and seeds of every kind,
Walnuts and almonds, guests will find.
Grasses and flowers and bulbs will abound,
Whatever the palate, every green will be found!"

So King Leo hurried and bustled about,
All would look perfect, no one had doubt.
Arranging each spot with the utmost of care,
Joy and excitement filling the air!

The Finest of Gold

When all was done he did summon his staff,
All were quite still, no one dared laugh.
"Now to invite all of our guests,
We will serve, only the best!

Envelopes sealed with the finest of gold,
Each quite unique, from the palace mold!
Here is the list, you plainly can see,
All cats are welcome to dine with me!

Ginger and Tulip, we must not forget,
Henry too, his place is set!
Dear old friends, we will meet,
All are quite special, each we'll greet.

We will dance and sing for joy,
We will laugh forevermore!
Love and joy will fill our hearts,
All will be a brand-new start!"

Each servant then prepared to go,
Garments pressed and tied with bows.

And when all was done, King Leo then sent,
His servants forth, and so they went.

Yet the rest of that day and as the sun did fall,
King Leo did think and ponder it all.

And when night did come, he went up to his bed,
While visions of laughter danced in his head!
Thinking of his palace feast,
Where he would serve cats, from greatest to least.

And so he looked into the night,
Gazing at the moon burn bright,
Watching stars sparkle white,
Waiting still for morning light.

Days of Warmth, Evening Chills

*E*arly with the break of day,
As beams of light cast their rays,
King Leo woke and quickly rose,
Wearing still his bedtime clothes!

Off he ran to have a look,
Shortest route is what he took!
Racing to the palace door,
Dashing over marble floors!

Carefully he took the latch,
Precisely he untied the catch.
Grasped the handle door quite tight,
Pulled the door with his great might.

Then he stood and gazed straight out,
Morning haze, round about.
Looking low and then up high,
For palace servants far or nigh.

"No one has returned to me,
That I can, clearly see.
Surely they will come quite soon,
Certainly before twelve noon!"

And so he pulled with his great might,
King Leo shut that door quite tight!
Took the latch and tied it so,
Turned around and then did go.

Crossing over marble floors,
Finally, at his bedroom door.
Pausing at the grand old clock,
As it chimed nine o'clock.

And so the hours passed away,
Now the sun, in full day,
Patiently he waited still,
Sitting at a window sill.

And then the sun began to set,
Casting shadows, windows let.
Dazzling colors scattered wide,
King Leo sat and gazed outside.

And when the dusk became dark night,
Still no servant was in sight.
King Leo rose and went to bed,
Baffled still, he scratched his head.

Now this went on for quite a while,
King Leo paced on palace tiles.
Marble halls, silent still,
Through days of warmth, and evening chills.

The grand old clock kept keeping time,
Tick-tock-tick would loudly chime.

Knock! Knock! Knock!

*T*hen one day King Leo sat,

Upon his gold, embroidered mat.

When suddenly a faraway—

Saw two servants clear as day!

King Leo stood and looked straight out,

Wiped his eyes, not one doubt!

"Could it be they've now returned?

And brought the answer that I've yearned?"

"Knock! Knock! Knock!" upon the door,
King Leo sped across the floor.
Grabbed the latch with his great might,
Held the handle very tight!

Pulled the door open wide,
Took one look and deeply sighed.
Standing there upon the step,
Stood two servants quite unkept.

"Come! Come! Come! Right inside—
Tell me all! Nothing hide!"

"His Majesty, indeed we went,
Every place, we were sent!
Offers clasped, in each hand,
Every place that you had planned!

Yet no matter where we set our feet,
None did welcome, none did greet.
We were amazed and quite surprised,
We truly felt much despised.

Although they knew where we were from,
Not one did want to even come!"

Then all at once, another knock,
All stood still, quite in shock.
"Pound! Pound! Pound!" the door did shake,
So strong the sound, the floor did quake!

King Leo then did grasp the latch,
Untied the cord, grabbed the catch.
Held the handle very tight,
Pulled that door with his great might!

And so the door opened wide,
King Leo stood, then deeply sighed.
There with heads hanging down,
Stood three servants, faces frowned!

"My, oh my, what is this?
Three more servants, all amiss!
Tell me now, what occurred?
I will note, every word!"

"His Majesty, the King, we tried,
Invite we did, far and wide!
But none did listen, nor would hear,
A word we spoke, we were quite clear!"

And this went on throughout the day,
Every servant, all did say,
"None would listen nor would hear,
Of your feast and welcome cheer!"

Another Thought

$\mathcal{K}$ing Leo sat, and then did muse,
Thinking just what to do!
"This is odd and strange to me,
None do listen or do see."

And then he had another thought,
"All this work, no not for naught!
I will try once again,
Other servants, I will send!"

King Leo then did call his staff,

New servants picked, on his behalf.

"Make sure to tell every guest,

Of my feast, the very best.

Fattened cattle, oxen slain,

All is set, why no delay!

I have prepared a glorious feast,

Come, partake, come take a seat!"

Yet before they left, or did depart,

He inspected, at the start.

Up, down, sideways too,

Studied well, from every view!

And when each one did look just right,
He gave a nod, very slight.
Stood and bid goodbye, farewell,
Prayed God's speed and bade them well.

"Go forth now, requests
        you bear,
Of my feast, you must share!"
And off they went, two by two,
To try again, much to do!

The Two Guards

$\mathcal{A}$nd so one day King Leo sat,
Upon his gold, embroidered mat.
In the palace dressing suite,
Waiting for the day to greet.

Windows open, brilliant light,
Sun shining, burning bright.

Sniffing air of lovely scents,
Lilac, rose, hyacinth.
Calming winds did gently blow,
Dreaming where the day may go!

Suddenly a noise occurred,
Voices loud, quite a stir!
Bursting through the chamber doors,
Dashed two guards on marble floors!

"His Majesty, the King, please pardon us,
We did not want to make a fuss.
But rush we did with news to share,
Wait, we simply could not bear!

We do bring words of grave import,
None before, of this sort!
Your servants have returned today,
They do appear quite dismayed!"

Yet while the guard, still did speak,
Came three servants, worn and weak!
One did limp upon a stick,
Every step did sound a crick.

Another wore a right arm sling,
Made of scraps and tattered string.
The last did bear a right eye patch,
Bound by cord with a catch.

All just stood, the clock did chime.
No one spoke, for quite some time.
King Leo looked at every one,
Each unkept and quite undone!

"Tell me now, about the rest,
And the answer of each guest!"

Suddenly the first did speak,
With all his might, still quite weak.
Took a step upon his stick,
Underneath, the ground did crick!

"His Majesty none would attend,
The words or message you did send.
Each went off upon his way,
To farm or business they would say!"

"But where right now are the rest?
I did send forth my very best!"

Quietly the second spoke,
Right arm sling, and a cloak.
Shook his head and then did sigh,
Tears of sadness filled his eyes.

"They did befall a dreadful fate,
Seized with force, and such hate!
We were mistreated, you can see,
Others killed yet we did flee!"

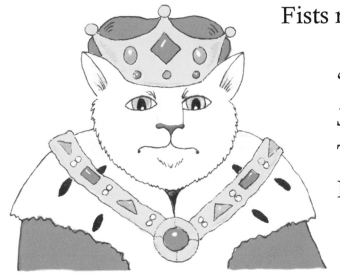

King Leo then had heard enough,
Enraged, his fur became quite gruff.
His eyes enlarged and opened wide,
Fists now clenched, at his side.

"What! Appalling! Can this be?
Just for cats to dine with me?
Truly I do not know why,
But surely this will not go by!

Assemble now my palace force,
Every soldier with his horse.
Bring to justice what occurred,
Defend my cause and make secure!"

And so, after just a while,
The army left, rank and file.

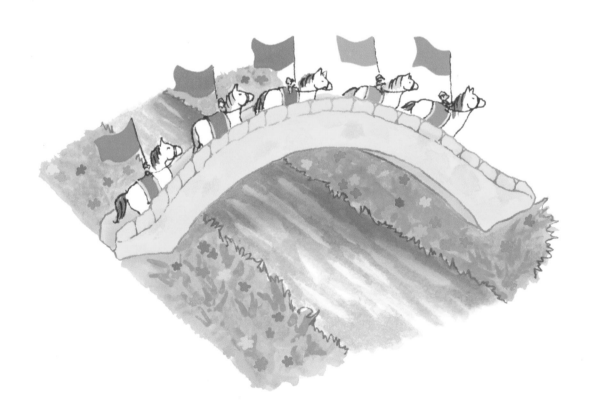

Dauntless, gallant in their stride,
Chasing culprits far and wide.
March they did, to the town,
In the city they were found.

They did slay those who caused such harm,
And burned their dwellings to the ground!

One and All

*K*ing Leo at the palace stayed,
   Skies now dark with clouds of gray,
   Servants standing all around,
   Faces gazing at the ground.

   King Leo paused and thought a while,
   Then with joy, he grandly smiled!
   His eyes did twinkle, sparkle bright,
   His voice was filled with delight!

"All is ready now to serve,
But those I chose did not deserve,
To partake of my feast,
Where is slain both ox and beast!

Go forth now and invite,
All you see, ignore all slight!
As many as you may find,
Bring them here to come and dine!

Highways, roads, where paths do meet,
By the way, be sure to greet!
Whatever house, lodge or home,
Cottage, dwelling or abode!

Highest peak or lowest cleft,
By the gates, not one left!
Lift your voice aloud and cry,
To everyone, far and nigh.

Your words are true, sound and just,
Proclaim to all, this you must!"

Astonished each was quite amazed,
Surprised and stunned, why in a daze!
Could it be, truly that,
They could invite just more than cats?

All were now quite astir,
Wondering what they just heard!
All began to chit-chat-chit,
And talk about every bit!

Then one servant did appear,
Tried to come up close and near!
Stepped right out, from the rest,
Strived to speak his very best!

"His Majesty, the King, please hear,
For a moment, please give ear!
Did you really, truly say,
We could invite all we may?

Small, large, short or tall,
Friend or foe, one and all?"

All servants suddenly did stop,
Inclined their ears, why jaws did drop!
Held their breath and came quite close,
Others stood upon their toes!

King Leo looked and thought awhile,
Glanced about, and then did smile,
Raised his voice loud and clear,
Then spoke, "Yes," for all to hear!

And with delight in one accord,
They all did shout, "Hooray," for joy!
All began to dance and sing,
And lift their voices with a ring!

Dashing Forth

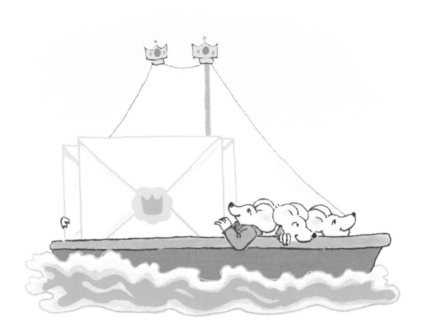

$\mathcal{E}$ach servant then did go his way,

Dashing forth, while still day!

Left, right, all about,

Cheerful, glad, not one pout!

Some went far, others near,

To share with any who would hear.

Land, sea, or oceans blue,

Off they went without ado!

Foot, horse, buggy, cart,
Any way, from the start!
To every place a map did show,
Even those that none did know!

One servant did go to a bay,
Where hippos lodged and did stay.
The servant asked, "Please come and dine,"
The hippos said, "Yes! Yes! How fine!"

And yet another one went forth,
Three blocks west and then four north!
Came upon a flock of sheep,
Grazing on a mountain steep!

The servant spoke of the spread,
Where all who came would be well fed.

The flock all voiced with cheer and glee,
Each did say, "Oh yes, me, me!"

Another came upon some grass,
Where giraffes did graze and others pass.
The servant beckoned with behest,
All did answer, "Yes! Yes! Yes!"

The servants did beseech and call,
The very great, and the small.
Everyone that they did meet,
All were welcome to come eat!

Zebras, cheetahs, monkeys too,
Lions and leopards and kangaroos!
All were asked to come partake,
Each said, "Yes," why none could wait!

Startled and Surprised

*A*nd then the day did swiftly come,
Sounds of flurry now a hum.
All was ready, quite complete,
All was set, every seat!

And so the sun in dazzling light,
Did chase dark clouds into night!
The palace trumpet then did sound,
Summoned guests from all around!

From sea to land to continent,
Every place the servants went.
Palace gates did open wide,
All began to come inside!

Then every guest did take their place,
The sun did shine upon each face!
Awe and wonder filled the air,
Sounds of glory, no more care!

Splendor captured it did seem,
Beauty far beyond a dream.

Soon the palace hall was filled,
Guests did feast on cattle killed.
Such food as this none had before,
All did ask for quite some more!

When suddenly King Leo gasped,
There did sit an unknown guest!
Clothed in garments from the street,
Not in dress for a feast.

"How was this soul seated here?
Where were the guards? Were none near?
Quick! We must make this right!
Surely before end of night!"

King Leo then did face the guest,
While still gazing at the rest,
Spoke directly to the soul,
"Friend, how did you come without right clothes?"

Speechless, startled, and surprised,
Despair and sorrow in his eyes.
He could not answer or reply,
Not a word, nor a sigh!

King Leo then turned to the guards,
His eyes with tears, heads all bowed,

"Take him out from the feast,
Where is slain both ox and beast.
Palace garments I prepared,
Which all must dress and all must wear."

The Greatest of Feasts

King Leo then did join the feast,
And did serve the great and least!
Zebras, cheetahs, monkeys too,
Lions and leopards and kangaroos!

Together they did laugh and dine,
Filled with joy, why each did shine!
"How wonderful to have such guests,
From North, South, East, and West!

Side by side, and unique,
Each quite special and distinct!
From every country, nation, tongue,
Every age, old and young!"

King Leo beamed, his face aglow,
His love for all did overflow!
Together they did sing for joy,
And laugh and dance forevermore!

About the Author

Gigi Amal is a Family Nurse Practitioner who currently resides with her family in the Midwest. She holds several degrees in healthcare yet has more recently begun to pursue her love of writing.

About the Illustrator

Theresa Burns has worked as a freelance illustrator for many years. She has illustrated 35 books, including two that she authored herself. Her books have received excellent reviews from *Publishers Weekly*, *School Library Journal*, and *Writer's Digest*. Theresa's paintings have sold in galleries throughout the United States, and she has painted murals in private homes, restaurants, schools and hospitals. She also works as a professional face painter and balloon artist. Theresa enjoys working with children and often visits schools to read her books and share her passion for illustration. Originally from Chicago, she now lives in Fort Lauderdale, Florida.

Order more books and other delightful items about *King Leo and the Feast* at

www.GigiAmal.com

CPSIA information can be obtained
at www.ICGtesting.com
Printed in the USA
LVHW071150181021
700739LV00001B/6